My Daddy Was a Soldier

☆   A World War II Story   ☆

I was five when World War II ended, but I still have clear memories of life on the home front and the knowledge that as a child, I lived through an important part of history.

Jeannie's experiences in this story are the kind that were shared by thousands of children. Many of those children, however, never saw their fathers again.

This book is dedicated to all the people who shared their stories of growing up in World War II with me.

Library of Congress Cataloging-in-Publication Data

Ray, Deborah Kogan
When daddy was a soldier / written and illustrated by Deborah
Kogan Ray. — 1st ed.
p.   cm.
Summary: While Daddy's away fighting in the Pacific, Jeannie
plants a Victory garden, collects scrap, and sends letters to her
father as she anxiously awaits his return.
ISBN 0-8234-0795-0
1. World War, 1939–1945—United States—Juvenile fiction.
[1. World War, 1939–1945—United States—Fiction.   2. Fathers—
Fiction.] I. Title.
PZ7.R21013Wh 1990
[E]—dc20   89-20056   CIP   AC

My Daddy
Was a Soldier

☆ A World War II Story ☆

written and illustrated by
Deborah Kogan Ray

Holiday House / New York

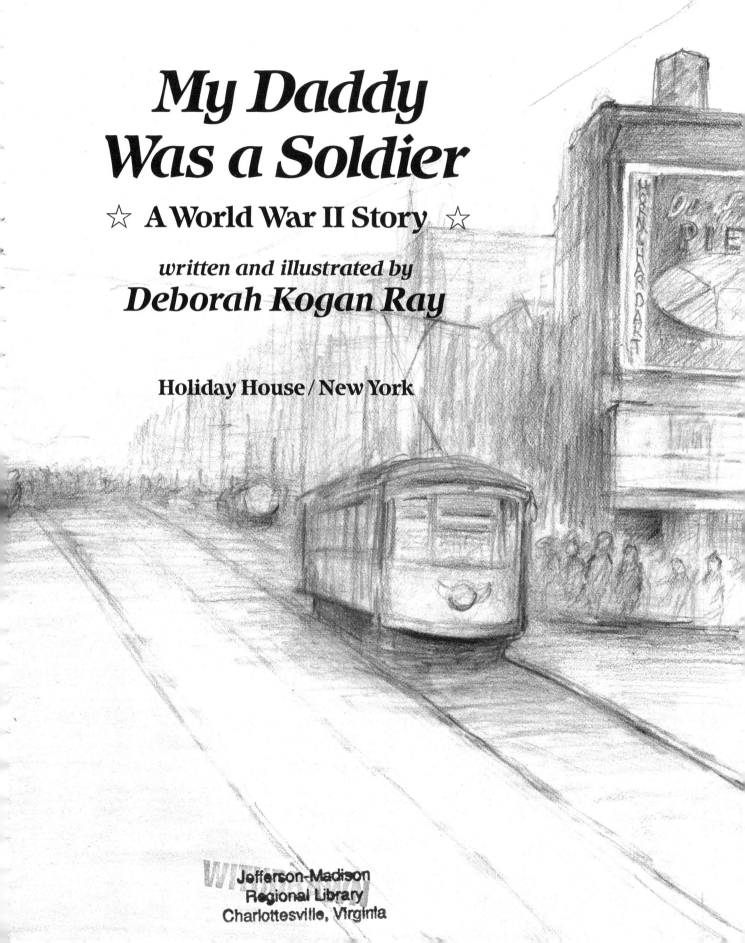

On December 7, 1941 the Japanese attacked Pearl Harbor in Hawaii. America went to war against Japan and Germany. Mama and Daddy and I listened to radio reports. We heard about terrible bombings and battles, but I felt safe in our house in Philadelphia. We were halfway around the world from the fighting.

Then things changed.

One by one the men on our street left to fight in the war. They were sent to fight in the Pacific, North Africa, and Italy.

In the spring of 1943, the war came into my house to take Daddy away. Daddy was going south to an army camp. From there we didn't know where he would be sent.

Mama and I went to the train station with Daddy to say good-bye. I tried to act brave, the way I thought a soldier's daughter should. But when I kissed Daddy, I cried until I thought my heart would break. Daddy hugged me tight. He promised to write letters to me. "You'll always be with me, Jeannie-o," he said. His voice sounded shaky and there were tears in his eyes.

That night I couldn't sleep, I missed Daddy so much.

Mama rocked me like a baby. She whispered, "We'll be getting a letter soon."

When Daddy's letter came three days later, I jittered until Mama opened it and read it aloud. Daddy wrote that he missed us very much. Then Mama and I sent a letter back. "We miss you too," Mama wrote in her neat, tiny script.

"Tell Daddy I wish he were home," I said. But I knew that he couldn't be, no matter how much I wished. Daddy was a soldier now. Home was Mama and me.

One morning Mama said, "Money's tight with Daddy gone. I'm going to get a job. There're lots of jobs for women now, doing work that men did before the war."

Mama went to work at the navy yard, using a welder to build big ships. I was proud of Mama, but the house felt big and empty when she left for work.

Every weekday morning she kissed me awake, then hurried to be on time for the early shift. I ate my cornflakes alone and watched the kitchen clock. It seemed like forever until it was time to leave for school.

After school I went to Mrs. Henry's house with other children whose mothers worked. I got the lonelies, even with the other children there. When it was time for Mama to come home, I ran to meet her at the trolley stop.

On Saturdays, Mama and I walked to Catherine Street to shop. Shopping was a big problem. Stores weren't open when Mama got home on weekdays and by Saturday, most of the stores had sold out of food.

The war had caused food shortages, since a lot of food was needed by our army and navy. America sent food to our friends in England, too. There wasn't much left for us at home. That's why our food was rationed. It could be bought only in small amounts. Everyone had to get ration books from the government. Each book had rows of stamps called points. There were blue points for canned goods and red ones for meats, cheese, and milk. They had to be used by a certain date or they weren't good anymore.

Mama and I walked from shop to shop. We waited in long lines, hoping there would be something left by the time we got to the counter. Most of the time, the butcher shop had a sign in the window that said "Closed—No Meat."

Mama bought as much canned "Spam" meat, canned vegetables, and canned fruits as she could find and our ration allowed. There were some things we could never get. There was no coffee for Mama and never any sugar on the shelves. Instead of sugar, we bought corn syrup. It tasted terrible on cornflakes.

Vegetables were scarce, too. President Roosevelt asked families to plant their own vegetable gardens. He called them "Victory gardens."

We planted our "Victory garden" behind the house. Our backyard was a narrow strip of hard dirt. We had never tried growing anything there. Mama and I scraped and dug until the ground was loose. We planted peas and beans and propped up tomato plants with sticks.

The garden smelled muddy sweet when we watered it. I watered it every day and pulled out weeds. Soon, tiny leaves sprouted up and the tomato plants started to grow.

I wrote to Daddy, "I wish you could see our victory garden. Mama and I had to put in taller sticks to hold up our tomato plants today. I can't wait to taste our very own tomatoes, but Mama says they won't be ready until the end of summer. Maybe the war will be over and you'll be home by then."

Daddy was sent across the country after he finished basic training. He got my letter when he was in San Diego. He wrote back that he hoped the war would be over soon, but he didn't think it would. "I'm waiting for orders that tell me where I'll be sent next," he wrote.

He enclosed a snapshot of himself. I thought he looked handsome in his uniform, but it made him look like a soldier. He didn't look like Daddy anymore.

Our next letter from Daddy had a different address. Daddy wrote "I've just gotten my orders. I'll board ship tomorrow morning. By the time you get this letter, I'll be on my way to fight the Japanese. I'm not allowed to tell you where I'm going. Keep writing letters, they'll be sent to me. I love you both and miss you very much."

When Mama finished reading, I didn't move. Daddy wasn't safe in America anymore. He was somewhere on the Pacific Ocean where there were terrible battles and ships being bombed.

I could hear my heart beating.

"Daddy might get killed," I said. Then I started to cry. Mama pulled me to her. She held me so tight, I could hardly breathe. She was crying, too.

Summer nights, Mama and the women on our street sat on the front steps and talked about the letters they had gotten from their husbands and sons.

Our soldiers were losing many of the battles. Sometimes the women's voices dropped to whispers. They were talking about someone who got wounded or killed.

There were lots of children on our street—twenty-seven around my age. Nearly everyone's father was away fighting. Some were fighting against the Germans in Europe. Some, like Daddy, were fighting in the Pacific against the Japanese.

We played "Kill the Enemy" around the parked cars. Our street was lined with cars that never went anywhere. Gasoline had been rationed because of the war. Only people with special jobs, like my best friend Carol's father, drove their cars.

Some nights there were blackouts. The air-raid siren would blast. The streetlights would dim and go out. We would pull down our shades and turn out our lamps. We practiced what to do, in case enemy planes came to bomb us. Everyone in the city had to turn out lights so that the enemy wouldn't find us.

In the pitch dark, I'd cuddle close to Mama in her bed and listen to the radio. Blackouts made the war feel real. I wondered if Daddy was afraid when real bombs fell from the sky.

The first day of school, our teacher, Miss Haggerty, told us that our class was going on the September "scrap drive." She said metal and rubber were in short supply and that everything we collected would be melted down and used to make things to help win the war.

"Be at the school yard ready to work," she said. "Remember, third graders, you can help the war effort, too."

Carol and I picked each other as a team. We couldn't wait to go. We'd never been old enough to do anything this important to help win the war.

Saturday morning, we and the other third graders lined up with our wagons. So did all the fourth, fifth, and sixth graders.

I said, "Carol, there are going to be too many kids around here. We're never going to get any scrap."

We decided to go farther than the other kids and headed up Chestnut Street. We had never been so far from home.

It was scary to go up and ring doorbells, but everybody had some old stuff to give us. Our wagons were clanking with pots and pans.

It was a long walk back to the school yard. We worried that we would be too late for the weigh-in, but we made it on time. And we won first prize for collecting the most pounds of metal scrap! We each got a box of fat school crayons and a certificate.

The crayons were a wonderful prize. Like all toys, they were scarce because of the war. My old crayons were worn to nubs. Mama hung my certificate on the kitchen wall and wrote a letter that night to Daddy about what I'd done.

A few weeks later, Carol told me her brother Patrick was coming home from the war. She said he was a wounded hero and had won medals for being so brave. I helped her hang crepe-paper streamers for his welcome home party.

Patrick arrived on crutches. His army pants were folded up and pinned where one leg had been. I tried not to look.

That night I had a bad dream. In my dream, I saw Daddy with one leg. Mama said Daddy wasn't hurt, but the bad dream wouldn't go away.

We usually got mail from Daddy once a week, though sometimes we got a recent letter before we got one that had been written weeks before. Often, letters came in bunches. Mama said that was because the letters had to wait to get picked up by ship and mail could pile up that way.

Right before Halloween, Mama and I took our Christmas presents for Daddy to the post office. I could tell by the extra heavy wrappings that everyone in the long line had a serviceman's package to mail.

Mama and I had baked cookies for Daddy. I'd drawn a picture with my crayons of Mama in her new Betty Grable movie star hairdo. I'd worked hard to make it look just right. I'd folded my picture carefully, and we'd packed it into the cookie tin. Packages couldn't be too big.

We were hoping for a Christmas letter from Daddy. I knew he couldn't send presents, like we could. But nothing came.

I tried not to cry on Christmas morning, but I couldn't help it. I missed Daddy so much. It didn't feel like Christmas without him there.

"I wish we'd gotten a letter," I said.

"I miss Daddy, too," Mama said. "There must have been so many soldiers sending letters home for Christmas, all the mail couldn't get here on time."

The day after Christmas, there still wasn't a letter. I was worried. Something had to be wrong. Five more days went by and no letters came.

Mama made me warm sweet milk to help me get to sleep. Still, I tossed and turned and woke up in the middle of the night because my dream about Daddy with one leg came back.

"Try to sleep, Jeannie," Mama whispered. "If something happened to Daddy, the army would have told us."

On the last day of the year, the first snowfall of winter turned our street into a white world. All morning, my friends rang our doorbell and asked me to come build snowmen and go sledding.

Mama said, "Go out and play, Jeannie."

But I wouldn't. "I have to wait for the postman," I said. I was shoveling the sidewalk, when I heard the postman call, "I've got something here for you, Jeannie. It looks like that letter you've been asking about."

I dropped the shovel and grabbed the letter from him. I didn't even say thank you.

"Mama, it's from Daddy! And it's for me," I called.

Daddy had sent me a picture of a decorated Christmas tree with a shining star on top, just like ours. He had drawn it himself. Below he had written "Merry Christmas, Jeannie-o; I wish I was home opening presents with Mama and you."

I put my letter in my special saving place in the top drawer of my dresser.

That night, I stayed up with Mama listening to the New Year's celebration at Times Square on the radio. At midnight, Mama kissed me and I kissed her.

"Happy New Year, 1944, Mama," I said.

I hoped that this year the war would end and Daddy would come home.

It was more than a year before the war in Europe finally ended. Germany surrendered in the spring of 1945. That summer, the United States dropped the most terrible bombs the world had ever known on two cities in Japan called Hiroshima and Nagasaki. Thousands of women and children died. After the A-Bomb, Japan surrendered.

V-J Day. Victory over Japan. Flags went up. People paraded and horns honked. Fireworks exploded in the sky. Mama took me to the celebration downtown. You couldn't move. Everybody was kissing everybody. I didn't know there were so many people in the world.

"We won. We won," I yelled with everybody else, until I was hoarse.

World War II was over. There would be no more fighting or bombing, no more worrying about whether Daddy would be all right.

That September I started fifth grade and waited for Daddy to come home.

In December, Daddy called from Chicago. He told Mama he was arriving the next day on the three o'clock train. I was so excited that I stayed up all night. Mama and I got to the train station early. A big sign was hanging over the door that said "Peace on Earth— Christmas 1945." The waiting room was crowded with families meeting servicemen. Christmas lights glittered from the ceiling and a school choir was singing Christmas carols by the information desk.

Mama grabbed my hand. She pointed to the train board. It was showing that Daddy's train had arrived.

A crowd of soldiers rushed up the stairs from the train. Then Daddy was there, scooping us into a big bear hug, kissing us, lifting me high in the air.

"Jeannie-o, how you've grown," he laughed.

I was laughing and crying at the same time.

Daddy held me tight. His uniform jacket was scratchy and the battle ribbons over his pocket hurt my cheek, but I wanted to stay there forever.

"You were always with me, Jeannie-o," Daddy said.

The war was over.

Daddy was home.